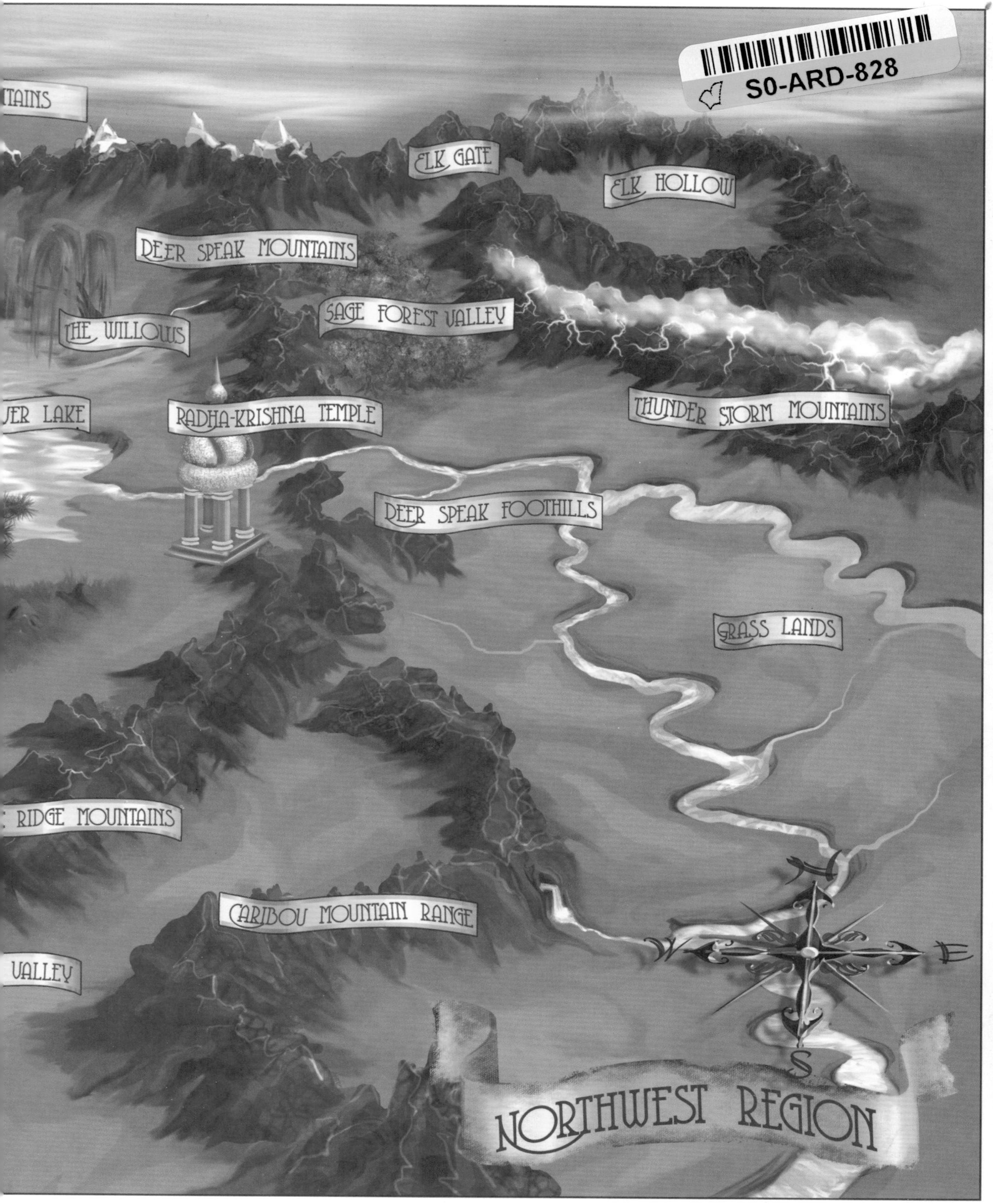

MOUNTAINS

ELK GATE

ELK HOLLOW

DEER SPEAK MOUNTAINS

SAGE FOREST VALLEY

THE WILLOWS

THUNDER STORM MOUNTAINS

...ER LAKE

RADHA-KRISHNA TEMPLE

DEER SPEAK FOOTHILLS

GRASS LANDS

...RIDGE MOUNTAINS

CARIBOU MOUNTAIN RANGE

...VALLEY

NORTHWEST REGION

KRISHNA BEDTIME STORIES

Volume One

Before the Beginning

Dharma Design Publications
1241 Adams Street
Suite 1000
St. Helena, CA 94574

www.krishnabedtimestories.com

Printed in China

This book is printed on 100% acid-free paper and the binding is reinforced.

Library of Congress Cataloging-in-Publication Data

Damodara, 1952-
Krishna bedtime stories. Volume one, Before the
beginning / retold by Damodara ; illustrated by Radhika.
p. cm.
Summary: Father Parrot teaches the animals of Tamel
Forest about Krishna and His spiritual world, and
Guardian Dova uses a story to teach them obedience.
Audience: Ages 5-12.
ISBN 0-9763541-0-1

1. Krishna (Hindu deity)—Juvenile fiction.
[1. Krishna (Hindu deity)—Fiction. 2. Forest animals—
Fiction. 3. Spirituality—Fiction. 4. Obedience—
Fiction.]   I. Radhika, 1952- II. Title. III. Title:
Before the beginning.

PZ7.S82614Kri 2006   [E]

Most of the information in the Krishna Bedtime Stories series about Krishna, His asso-
ciates, pastimes, philosophy, etc., comes from the books, lectures, letters and conversa-
tions of His Divine Grace A.C. Bhaktivedanta Swami Prabhupada, the world-renowned
exponent of the science of Krishna consciousness in the West and beyond, recognized
by numerous respected scholars as an eminently brilliant teacher of Vedic religion
and thought. Some of the descriptions in the series, mainly in Volume One, have been
gleaned from authorized Vedic texts belonging to the spiritual lineage he represents.

10 9 8 7 6 5 4 3 2 1

KRISHNA BEDTIME STORIES

Volume One

Before the Beginning

Retold by Damodara dasa

Illustrated by Radhika dasi

Dharma Design
Publications

St. Helena, California

This book belongs to
Komathy . Mohan
Shamira, Karishma + Pg hy.

Dedicated to all children on whose wisdom the future of this planet depends.

Contents

Preface

The most important questions in life are commonly considered through the culture, religion or philosophy of one's upbringing. Based on the wisdom and teachings of India's esteemed, ancient Vedic literature, the Krishna Bedtime Stories series attempts to provide parents a way to consider with their children answers to some of life's biggest questions: Who are we? Where do we come from? Why are we here on this earth? Why should we be "good"? Why do good people suffer? How can we find peace and happiness? Where do we go when we die?

It was through the late George Harrison's compelling devotional songs—such as "Govinda" and "My Sweet Lord," which conclude with the chanting of beautiful, sacred Vedic mantras—that I was first introduced to the *Vedas* and their teaching of the Supreme Lord Krishna.

My interest in (and appreciation for) the *Vedas* was reinforced by frequent references to them in the contemporary writings of such notable scientific thinkers as Stephen Hawking, Carl Sagan, Joseph Campbell and Deepak Chopra.

As I studied the *Vedas* for myself, my growing enthusiasm led me to share what I was learning with my young children in a way that they could appreciate.

That is how the idea for the Krishna Bedtime Stories was conceived. Their birth and development has been, for my family and me, a blessed journey of discovery and delight.

My fond hope is that this labor of love will provide many rewarding and pleasurable hours for you and your children, awakening in them a desire to explore the profound, timeless knowledge contained in India's vast treasure house of sublime Vedic literature.

Sincerely,

Damodara dasa

Krishna and His Home
Chapter One

A long time ago, almost before memory, deep in the forest called Tamel, there lived a mother and father parrot. A large branch had broken off high up a towering pine tree leaving a wound in its magnificent trunk—a natural hollow—that provided the perfect home for the colorful, long-lived birds.

From their home in the great tree that had come to be called Parrot Pine, Mother and Father Parrot enjoyed a spectacular view of the mountains whose shadows encircled their forest. From their elevated post the parrots had—what else—a bird's-eye view of the river that leaped and laughed its way across thousands of smooth stones into a refreshing blue lake where Mother Deer regularly led her fawns to drink at the water's edge.

Any time of day, using their keen sight and sharp sense of hearing, the parrot pair enjoyed the colors and the songs of so many other birds, the chatter of monkeys swinging among the trees, squirrels jumping from limb to trunk and the scurrying of smaller animals along the lush forest floor.

Father and Mother Parrot were blessed with three very healthy baby parrots who laughed and played with each other as only young parrots can. Their names were Penelope, Peter and Paul.

One afternoon while Father Parrot, the mayor of Tamel Forest, was searching for food, Winslow, the wise old owl who lived alone in a nearby oak tree, got the attention of his noisy neighbors. After spinning his head around in every direction, he suggested in a quiet whisper to the young parrots that they ask their father to tell them the secrets of the great spiritual world beyond.

"Great spiritual world beyond?" they asked. The triplets looked at each other with widening eyes. It had never occurred to them that there was a world beyond Tamel Forest, or that they were not necessarily the very center of it all.

Young parrots are much like young people: they want to be in on any secret, especially very important ones. So when Father Parrot returned from foraging for food he got a begging from his children. "Tomorrow evening," he promised, "I will begin to tell you about the spiritual world beyond our forest that always has been and always will be overflowing with happiness." He had been planning to tell them about this soon and was pleased to see their interest.

The triplets slept less soundly that night, and the next morning they awoke in time to hear the earliest birds welcome the day. They were excited, waiting to enjoy the promised story of the great secret their father would be telling that very evening. They wanted their many forest neighbors to hear the story too, so they squawked at the top of their young lungs to anyone who would listen.

Winslow the Owl chuckled to himself about the excitement he had started. Now and then he had told various forest animals that he and his close friend, Father Parrot, had for many years studied the great mysteries of the spiritual world beyond their forest. Most of the animals had passed it off as the exaggerations of an aging bird. But now, as the sun settled low and the trees made shadows like long paths on the forest floor, they began to gather at the top of the curved rocky cliff that rose toward the sky just behind Parrot Pine. Raccoons, chipmunks, deer, eagles, swallows, foxes—even river otters, who were rarely serious about anything, left the lake to sit quietly with their land-bound friends.

This gathering of so many members of the forest community impressed the parrot triplets with not only how important the story must be, but with how important their father must be. Truth be told, they felt a little puffed-up and superior.

Father Parrot returned to Parrot Pine with his beak full of tasty nuts and berries. As he flew into the setting sun shining brightly in his eyes, he did not notice until the last moment the large crowd that had gathered on the great cliff before Parrot Pine. He recognized immediately that someone (or more likely, some ones) had spread the word that he was planning to tell the story of the spiritual world and its creator.

Father Parrot landed on Parrot Pine, entered his home and emptied his beak of the goodies he had gathered. After preening a couple of stray feathers, he stepped out onto the modest tree limb near the entrance to his hollow. He gazed out over the gathering of his many diverse neighbors, glanced lovingly toward his wife, the triplets and then back to the waiting animals.

"Nice of you all to drop by," he joked. "Usually we just have our three young parrots for story time at Parrot Pine—and they tend to be restless." Father Parrot then became a bit serious saying, "I realize that you each came to hear something important, and in the little time we have until dark, I'm happy to begin sharing with you what I know about the things that matter most."

There were murmurs all around from the forest animals that meant, "Thank you!"

Father Parrot began by describing a very large planet in the spiritual world that is high above all the rest and is the home of God, His friends and loved ones. "God's name is Krishna, which means that He is the most attractive person in all ways."

As Father Parrot began to describe Krishna, the imaginations of the young parrots (and those of all the animals) went in dizzying directions. Father Parrot explained, "Krishna is an attractive youth whose skin is a beautiful bluish color, as pleasing as a cooling rain cloud. He has black, curling hair, and the palms of His hands and the soles of His feet are a wonderful reddish color. He always carries a flute that is decorated with sparkling gemstones. At each end of Krishna's golden flute are lovely rubies that shine in the light."

One feature of Krishna's magical flute reminded the animals of some of their forest friends. "It changes its color, depending on which part of Krishna it is touching," explained their story-telling mayor. "When Krishna touches the flute to His teeth, it appears like a crystal wand. When the flute touches His reddish palms, it appears like a ruby stick. And when the flute touches Krishna's handsome blue cheek, it appears to be made of sapphire." Upon hearing this, some of the lizards in the audience–the chameleons, who can change the color of their bodies–rose up proudly on their hind legs and looked around to see who might be noticing them.

Father Parrot, seeing them, smiled and said, "The music that Krishna plays on His flute is so sweet and enchanting that it fills the animals living in His home with spiritual happiness."

The parrot triplets were amazed by the thought of spiritual happiness and wanted to become filled with it. But this evening they were too shy, in front of such a large audience of grown-ups, to interrupt with loud questions as they normally did when their father told them a story.

"As each of you listen to the stories I tell, your ears will begin to hear the sound of Krishna's flute, even while you remain in this forest of our material world," Father Parrot explained.

By this time it wasn't just the triplets who wanted to speak. Sarah the Swan was so pleased by what Father Parrot had described that she raised her large white wing and said, "I have heard whispers for many years that it is possible to hear the sound of Krishna's flute, and I'm eager to learn how to listen for it."

The other animals were also intrigued by what the learned parrot had described to them about Krishna, so Father Parrot continued. "He always wears one rainbow-colored peacock feather just above His forehead. Krishna is so attractive that even Cupid finds Him charming."

Several young bluebirds were listening in a nearby tree. Billy the Bluebird called out, "Mayor Parrot, who is Cupid?" Before he answered the question, Father Parrot asked the bluebird youngsters if their mother had given them permission to come so far from home alone.

"Yes," said Billy, "Mother said this would be the most important story we could ever hear. She is home with our little sister who is sick; but she let us come on two conditions: that we listen carefully and that we fly home before it is completely dark."

Father Parrot liked his answer and explained, "Cupid is the most attractive being within the material world in which we live." With that brief explanation he returned to his description of Krishna.

"Krishna's spiritual, effulgent body smells more wonderful than the sweetest jasmine flowers in our world," explained Father Parrot. "From His waist to His ankles He wears a gold-colored robe, called a *dhoti*, and earrings that match." Many of the animals were closing their eyes trying to see the beautiful picture of Krishna in their minds. Father Parrot continued to describe the pearl necklace that Krishna wears—pearls as white as snow—and the colorful flower garlands He wears around His neck.

For some reason, the mention of garlands excited a very friendly chipmunk known as Chandler. He raced to the high end of a fallen tree and hollered a deal to Father Parrot. Chandler promised that he and the other chipmunks would make garlands of forest flowers for all the animals who would come to Parrot Pine tomorrow evening, if the mayor would continue telling them the secrets of Krishna and His planet in the spiritual world.

Of course Father Parrot was willing to do so, even without Chandler's eager promise of garlands; but he thanked the chipmunk for his thoughtful and generous offer before concluding with a bit more about Krishna's magnificent home.

"Krishna lives on the topmost planet in the spiritual world," Father Parrot said. "His planet is called Goloka Vrindavan, which means 'The Planet of the Cows.'"

"Cows?" the forest animals asked, as they squinted, frowned and tilted their heads. They had never seen or heard of cows before.

Recognizing their confusion, Father Parrot said, "A cow very much resembles an ox or a caribou." That was helpful. The forest friends imagined a caribou as Father Parrot continued to speak about Goloka Vrindavan—the planet created by the mystical powers of Krishna.

"Goloka Vrindavan is a planet filled with the greatest spiritual happiness. Everyone who lives there with Krishna is filled with this spiritual joy," said Father Parrot, smiling at the thought. "There is no such thing as death in Goloka Vrindavan, as there is here in our forest; because of this, no fear or worry exists there either."

The animals were amazed at the thought of such a place. Father Parrot continued, explaining that on Goloka Vrindavan there are many forests in which thousands of *tulsi* plants grow, and that these *tulsi* plants are very dear to Krishna.

Father Beaver raised his paw to ask Father Parrot, "Is that why you often go to visit the *tulsi* plants way down below Cave Maker Valley?"

"That's right," said Father Parrot. "I fly down there at least once a week to pay my respects to the sacred *tulsi* plants."

The forest animals were happy to think that a plant that grows on Goloka Vrindavan—a plant so special to Krishna— also grew near their forest. Percival, one of several peacocks in the crowd, told Father Parrot that all of the animals who were present wanted to know more about Krishna's spectacular home.

"Well," said Father Parrot, as he squinted to check the light remaining in the sky, "everything on Goloka Vrindavan is fully alive and conscious, including the trees, plants, flowers, mountains, grass, waterfalls, ponds of water—even the sparkling dust on the ground." This was a complicated new idea for the forest animals, something they had never heard of before; but Father Parrot helped them understand it by telling them that what it really means is that everything on Goloka Vrindavan is able to think and communicate with everything else.

And there was more. "All of the living beings on Goloka Vrindavan have pure hearts," said Father Parrot. He did not mean that they have material bodies with hearts inside them that pump blood. Rather, he meant that they have spiritual bodies, like Krishna Himself, and are all filled up inside with love for Krishna and for one another. "No one on Goloka Vrindavan becomes jealous, angry or greedy," said Father Parrot, speaking of the feelings that sometimes damaged friendships among the animals of Tamel Forest. (Just a few days earlier Ruben the Raccoon and Grady the Goose had fought over a red, juicy apple that had fallen from a nearby tree. Father Parrot noticed the young friends were present and listening.)

"On Goloka Vrindavan, children are naturally kind to their friends and obedient to their parents," said Father Parrot smiling at his triplets.

Noticing that the sky was darkening, Father Parrot realized he needed to bring the story to a good stopping point. "I want you to know that what I have been telling you tonight is not a fairy tale or simply my imagination," he said.

"The more you hear these stories about Krishna, the more you will long to go to the spiritual world to be with Him. You will also become more obedient, honest and kind. This will help us live in harmony together."

With that, Father Parrot bowed slightly and waved a wing to say good night.

The Divine Couple

Chapter Two

The three baby parrots slept so well that night they awoke late the next morning, startled by a bright and fully risen sun. The youngsters each told their parents how well they had slept and how rested they felt. As she fed her children their breakfast, Mother Parrot told them that the more they learned about Krishna, the easier it would become for them to feel safe as they went to sleep each evening.

It was just an ordinary day until late in the afternoon. Father Parrot was sitting on a tree limb, thinking about what he was going to say that evening, when he noticed a group of beavers waddling up a path from the Blue Fork River toward Parrot Pine. He had never seen the beavers appear so energetic and alive. Their necks were nicely decorated with garlands fashioned from colorful forest flowers.

Father Parrot swooped down close to where they were walking to learn their destination. Father Beaver answered: "Chandler the Chipmunk and his family invited us to the fire pits where, on their roasting stones, they cook tasty roots and nuts for themselves and other forest animals. They also showed us the many flower garlands they had made. Since we are so much bigger, they asked us to take the garlands and hang them on branches near the edge of the rocky ridge that stands near Parrot Pine. That way the garlands will be ready to give to the animals who come to hear the next telling of the Krishna stories."

"Mercy me," said Father Parrot. "I never thought that Chandler and his family would put this much effort and art into making so many gorgeous flower garlands. I know that the animals will love wearing them this evening, as they learn more about the spiritual world and Krishna. Wearing these garlands will remind us that Mother Nature and all her beauty come from Krishna."

A second beaver broke in to say, "We will need to make one more trip to the chipmunks' fire pits. Chandler and his family roasted many different kinds of nuts early this morning. This will allow the animals to have a tasty treat to snack on following your story about Krishna and His world this evening."

"What a good idea," said Father Parrot. "This will make our evening even more special. The animals will hear about the spiritual world, their tongues will taste the roasted nuts, their eyes will see the colorful flower garlands and their noses will smell the delightful fragrance. When the animals pass by the two marble blocks waiting to be carved into graceful images, they will feel the cool, hard Gemini marble."

"What images?" the youngest beaver inquired in a high voice.

Father Parrot asked the young beaver to be patient, because he wanted the answer to be a surprise for the evening story. Then he asked if the beavers would be willing to do something very important for the Tamel Forest community.

The busy mammals looked at each other, curious, pleased and cautious all at once. "We would love to do whatever we can to help," said Father Beaver, "but before we make a promise we would like to know what we are agreeing to do."

"You are very wise," said Father Parrot. "I agree that it is important to always know exactly what you are promising before you give your word." And so he told the beavers that he wanted them to help build a temple. "I will give you the design and plans from which you can work. I will also have elephants bring large logs cut from teakwood trees—the hardest wood in our region. With your help," he finished his request, "we will build a noble temple in Tamel Forest where we can worship Krishna."

Although beavers are the forest's lumberjacks, carpenters and dam builders, Father Beaver told Father Parrot that his request was a large one and he would need to call the other beavers in their lake together to discuss the project. They would decide among themselves, he said, whether they had enough beavers with the time and talent to do the job well. But he promised to give Father Parrot an answer before the meeting started that evening.

Father Parrot thanked the beavers for helping the chipmunks. He asked them to keep an eye on the roasted nuts until the evening's story was completed, so that other animals, who might smell the nuts and get the munchies, wouldn't try to eat the treats before the right time. This was an easy promise for the beaver bunch to make.

As the group continued to the ridge, Father Beaver headed for the lake where he cracked his powerful, broad tail loudly on the water as he did when he wanted to call a meeting.

The young parrots watched from their high nest as the beavers delivered the flower garlands and nuts to the rocky cliff before Parrot Pine. Paul, the smallest of the young parrots, sang out to Father Parrot, "Thank you for teaching us last night and for letting so many of our forest friends come and listen." The other two baby parrots, Penelope and Peter, also chimed in with their thanks.

"I was glad to tell the story and even happier that you and so many other forest friends are interested in learning about Krishna," Father Parrot said with a smile, as he flew away on a short errand.

Soon after this, some older parrots flew carefully from the other side of the lake, landing near the hollow in Parrot Pine. After greeting their young relatives, they asked them about the rumor they had heard regarding their father—that he had told the most fascinating story the night before to quite a gathering of forest friends, and that he might have more to tell this very evening.

"Oh, yes!" squawked the little parrots enthusiastically, adding, "You, and anyone you know, are welcome to come."

The senior parrots were pleased. "Fantastic," said one of them who had a few graying feathers. "We will fly back to The Willows and tell the rabbits, because we know they would love to come."

"Goody! We will tell our father," said the baby parrots, as the old parrots were lifting off, flapping their wings in the sky across Beaver Lake toward their home in a tree near The Willows.

Soon Father Parrot returned with food for Mother Parrot, who divided it among her three children's upturned mouths. After dinner, Mother Parrot prepared them for the very special evening by grooming their feathers and polishing their beaks.

With the sun fading into evening, the Tamel Forest animals began to gather again on the rocky ridge atop the cliff by Parrot Pine, settling themselves rather quietly for more of the Krishna stories. No sooner had Father Parrot welcomed his guests than Mother Raccoon offered to prepare an after-story treat for the next evening. "The thickets are just loaded with fat, juicy blackberries," she announced. "My children and I will pick enough for everyone tomorrow evening."

"Wonderful," said Father Parrot. The three little parrots looked at each other and giggled with excitement.

Father Parrot glanced at them as he began to thank their chipmunk friends for providing roasted nuts for everybody to enjoy on their journey home. He also told everyone who had not been able to hear that Mother Raccoon and her young ones were bringing berries the next evening. This pleased all the animals, who were hoping that tonight would not be the end of the stories.

Standing near Father Parrot, Mother Parrot added, "Not only did Chandler the Chipmunk and his large family of small chipmunks prepare tasty roasted nuts for after the story, they also worked very hard making lovely flower garlands for each of us. So if everyone will now go to the branches holding the garlands, someone will place one around each of your necks. As you listen to tonight's story," she added, "you can remember that Krishna loves to wear garlands made of flowers."

"Thank you, chipmunks, thank you!" came many voices from the ridge.

"Thank you! Thank you!" came other voices from nearby branches.

As the garland wearing forest crowd returned to their places, Father Parrot began speaking, "Last evening I described Krishna and Goloka Vrindavan, the planet where He lives." He moved his claws for a more comfortable grip. "From time to time I will add marvelous, new details of God and the planet He lives on. But tonight I want to tell you about Krishna's companion named Radharani."

This was very intriguing; the animals' ears twitched with interest. "Krishna and Radharani are always together," said Father Parrot. "Radharani smells sweeter than the most fragrant flowers. She is very charming and She never grows old because Her body is completely spiritual, just like Krishna's," Father Parrot explained.

"Radharani loves to play beautiful music for Krishna's pleasure," Father Parrot continued. "The animals on Goloka Vrindavan love to hear Radharani play Her vina, a stringed musical instrument, while Krishna plays His flute. The music they make together holds the animals in awe.

"Radharani is patient, playful, respectful and shy. She is considered to be the greatest devotee of Krishna."

"What is a devotee?" Penelope shyly asked her father as she carefully leaned out of their hollow.

Father Parrot turned to look lovingly at his young ones and answered, "A devotee of Krishna is someone who loves Him with his or her whole heart and soul."

Father Parrot explained, "Radharani shows us through Her example how easy it is to love Krishna."

Everyone was listening carefully as Father Parrot described Radharani. But it was Pearl, the wife of Percival the Peacock, who asked with her soft voice, "Please tell us more about their relationship."

Father Parrot nodded. "Words cannot describe how close Krishna and Radharani are to each other. If everyone would look to Them as an example, there would be nothing but love in every home. This is why They are called the Divine Couple by the residents of the spiritual world. Krishna loves Her so much that He wears a locket on His chest that contains a picture of Her."

"How special," whispered Pearl.

"By the way," said Father Parrot, smiling, "Radharani is also known by another name. Many devotees in this world call Her Mother Hara. She is especially respectful, patient and affectionate to elderly people."

Father Parrot decided it was time to reveal what was planned for the pair of marble blocks that stood near the limbs on which their flower garlands were hung earlier that evening. He asked his forest friends to notice their two different colors: one was an unusually stunning blue, and the other was gold.

"As you leave," he said, "you may walk over and feel them before they are carved into Radharani and Krishna. We will place them in the center of Tamel Forest's first temple."

"Temple? What's a temple?" came the voice of Stripeford the Skunk, one of two striped skunks standing near the raccoons.

"A temple is a sacred building that shelters Radharani and Krishna," said Father Parrot. "I have asked the beavers if they would be willing to use their carving tools and skills to make a sacred temple from teakwood. This temple will become the abode of Radharani and Krishna. And just before our story tonight, the beavers agreed to provide this difficult but important and joyful service."

Father Beaver stood up, balanced by his strong tail, and said, "Speaking for the Tamel Forest beavers, we are honored to help with the new temple project."

"And I am grateful to you for agreeing to do so," Father Parrot said, bowing respectfully in Father Beaver's direction.

"This morning I flew over the Deer Speak Mountains in search of Eli the Orangutan, an elderly student of an advanced devotee of Krishna called Old Gray Elk," Father Parrot announced. "As you may know, the orangutans living in the Sage Forest Valley build a new nest made of branches and leaves high in the trees to rest in each night.

"What you may not know is that Eli the Orangutan has shaped some of the most magnificent statues in our region," said Father Parrot. "I was worried about finding him, because he travels so much; but I was lucky. When I found him, another student of Old Gray Elk from the Sage Forest Valley was thanking him for creating a marble carving for their temple.

"I asked Eli if he would be willing to shape our marble blocks into Radharani and Krishna. At first he seemed reluctant; he felt that his hands were getting too weak and tired to continue the quality of work for which he is known. But the student who was visiting asked him to agree to my request. Due to the amount of respect that Eli has for his visiting friend, he agreed to start working on the marble next week," Father Parrot announced with relief.

As the meeting was ending, the enthusiasm among the animals was observed by Father Parrot. He had explained so many new and different things in such a short time. The thought of actually having a temple in Tamel Forest was so great it gave energy to everyone present.

"What a wonderful evening," said Percival the Peacock, as he respectfully lowered his large tail of colorful feathers. "I am grateful that you spent this time teaching us." Then, as he prepared to bow, he said in a loud voice, "Good evening, everyone!"

"Good evening," Father Parrot replied as he turned and smiled to his attentive guests, his three children and his wife.

The Falcon Alert
Chapter Three

"What's that sound?" asked a small raccoon with alarm.

"I hear it," said another young raccoon, suddenly alert.

"Me too," worried their brother, Ruben, "and it's getting closer."

"Look over there," said Mother Raccoon, as she pointed west toward the top of the Tiger Ridge Mountains.

Flying in the direction of Marmore Marsh where the raccoons lived was a falcon racing down from the mountain peaks at a speed very few birds could fly. The noise that alarmed the raccoons was the falcon screeching at the top of its lungs, "Help! Get the medics. Help! Where are the medics?"

"The falcon is headed for the animal medical clinic near Beaver Dam," Mother Raccoon said, peering across the lake. "Someone must be hurt."

"Who is that bird?" asked Ruben.

"That's Danbar the Falcon," Mother Raccoon replied. "He is the flying ranger who uses his keen sight and great speed to protect the animals over the whole Northwest Region. Something has happened. Something terrible has happened!" she emphasized.

With a great spreading of his feathers, Danbar the Falcon landed suddenly on a tree branch in front of the animal medical clinic.

"Help! Help! A baby tiger has been wounded by a hunter in the foothills of the Tiger Ridge Mountains above Tiger Tooth Valley," Danbar hollered.

The chief medic, a bright young doe, pointed toward two sturdy-looking deer standing nearby, tightening down the emergency gear on their backs.

"They're ready to leave immediately," said the chief medic. "Don't get too far ahead of them. Make sure they are able to follow you. The clouds are low today, and as you fly higher into the mountains they could lose sight of you."

The lead medic deer carried a medical emergency kit on her back; the other medic dragged a device behind her—something like a stretcher—called a travois.

The medic deer followed the path that wound past the tree where the baby parrots were peering out with concern, and continued toward the Oak Log Bridge that crossed over the Blue Fork River.

There was no time to waste as they started their climb toward the northwest. The clouds hung low around the mountain peaks. It was not clear whether the sun would burn the moisture away, or if there would be rain in the afternoon.

As they reached the tops of the mountains, Danbar hollered down, "Over there. The baby tiger is on the other side of that crest."

Breathing heavily because she was very tired, the lead deer asked, "Is there any . . . danger still . . . present in . . . the area?"

"No," Danbar the Falcon replied. "The great white tigers scared the hunter back down across Tiger Tooth Valley and into the Bay Ridge Mountains."

"Good," panted the lead deer.

It was surprising how fast the healthy medic deer could travel, despite the rocky ground, heavy packs and trailing travois.

Just ahead, the falcon flew in a small circle over a rough but sparsely wooded area. The medics slowed down beneath Danbar's orbit and spotted the young tiger lying on his side. His heartbroken mother leaned over him, gently licking his face and head.

While the medic deer who had pulled the travois so far stood still catching her breath, the other medic, with Mother Tiger's help, lifted the small tiger onto the blanket.

As soon as the wounded cub, named Tully, was wrapped and tied securely to the travois, Mother Tiger came close and assured her son that the deer would keep him safe. She whispered to Tully that she and Father Tiger would arrange for someone to look after his little brother, so they could travel to visit him. She gave her precious son a few more loving licks before leaving him with the medics for the return journey to the medical clinic.

Danbar sat on a low tree branch near Mother Tiger. "We will do everything we can to make certain your baby gets the best possible care," he said. "We'll let you know about his condition sometime tonight."

"Thank you for taking care of Tully," said Mother Tiger with relief.

For the medic deer, time and landmarks passed very quickly. Soon they were running by Marmore Marsh and crossing over the Oak Log Bridge. As they neared the clinic they passed Parrot Pine again, where the baby parrots were worriedly peering out from their perch.

"What's going to happen?" Peter asked his mother.

"The chief medic will look at the baby tiger's wounds and decide what kind of treatment it needs," Mother Parrot whispered in a concerned tone. "They will then act quickly and carefully."

Just about that time Father Parrot landed next to his nest.

"Father, why do the tigers live up in the mountains?" asked Peter's brother, Paul.

"They live there to guard Tamel Forest and all the land to the east, from the two-legged creatures, called humans, who live in Blue Bay Village near the ocean," he replied. "These humans used to go hunting in the Bay Ridge Mountains to kill and eat the animals who lived there.

"An important arrangement was made many years ago with the mountain lions who lived in the Bay Ridge Mountains. The big cats agreed to become vegetarians—they would no longer kill and eat any animals. They also agreed to prevent the hunters from coming into their territory. In exchange for this service, the animals in Tiger Tooth Valley offered to give the mountain lions all the tasty vegetarian food they wanted." Father Parrot was in a teaching mood.

"The mountains between Tiger Tooth Valley and Tamel Forest are called the Tiger Ridge Mountains. A similar treaty was made with the great white tigers: they could live among those peaks and get all the delicious vegetarian food they could possibly want if they would capture any hunters who got past the mountain lions and the Bay Ridge heights. These creatures are so loyal to us that they would never willingly let any hunters get past them.

"Many years ago," Father Parrot continued, "Old Gray Elk, who lives beyond the Deer Speak Mountains in Elk Hollow, taught the mountain lions and the white tigers that it was better for them to eat the meat of an apple or bean, for example, than the flesh of other animals."

"Did the mountain lions and white tigers really eat other animals?" asked the baby parrots. They had never heard of animals eating other animals.

"Yes," Father Parrot said. "Animal flesh was their main source of food."

"Oooh!" said the baby parrots, shivering at the thought of being a tiger treat.

"It may take time," Father Parrot said, "but the day will come when the teachings of Old Gray Elk will persuade most humans to become vegetarians too."

Father Parrot told his fledglings that after they learned more about Krishna they would understand clearly why it's better for everyone to eat nuts, grains, fruits and vegetables, rather than to kill and eat the flesh of poor, innocent animals, causing them so much fear and pain.

The baby parrots really liked the idea of vegetarian cats, but for now they continued to worry about the tiger cub. "We just hope that the baby tiger will soon be okay and able to go home to its family," they all said.

After leaving for a short time to visit with the medics at the animal clinic, Father Parrot returned to his nest to tell his children that the young tiger's name was Tully. He also told them that although Tully had been hurt very badly by the hunter, he would soon regain his strength and mend. He promised to check in with the medics again just before that evening's gathering, so he could tell all the animals the latest news about Tully's recovery.

This was a great relief to the tired young parrots who were late for the naps they so badly needed to be ready for story time.

The Spiritual Sky
Chapter Four

As soon as Father Parrot saw the size of the crowd that was gathering on top of the cliff, it became clear to him that they could not continue their meetings in the same place. There were already too many guests and not enough room for everyone to listen comfortably—or safely.

All around, the animals could be heard talking about Tully, the wounded tiger cub. Many of them were wondering, "How did he get hurt, and will he live?"

Father Parrot said in his authoritative voice, "If I could have your attention, I would like to say a few things before our story begins. First of all, I want you to notice the size of the crowd that has gathered here tonight. As you can see, we have run out of room. So the next time we meet, it will be in the clover field southeast of The Willows. There should be plenty of room there, so please feel free to continue to join us and invite any of your family and friends to come."

Father Parrot then spoke about what had happened to Tully, for those who had not yet heard. He said he had just returned from meeting with the medic taking care of Tully who told him that the medical treatment of his wound had been successful. He also said the cub's parents would be coming down from the mountains to visit with him the next afternoon.

"Tully is very lucky," said Father Parrot. "The arrow shot by the hunter came within an inch of his heart. He should be back up on his paws and much stronger soon."

"How is it, Father Parrot, that the cub's body is able to heal so quickly?" asked Osmund, a young river otter.

"When you tear your jacket, your mother must examine it in order to mend it," Father Parrot answered. "The same is true with the tiger cub's body. The cub has already been taught by his parents that he is not his body; he is the spirit soul living inside his body. He knows that his body is just like a jacket or covering that he wears over himself–the spirit soul. The cub has learned that his spirit soul knows how to repair his body, just as his mother knows how to fix the jacket.

"The spirit soul is conscious or aware and is spread throughout every part of our physical body. Because we have consciousness, when someone pinches our arm we feel the pain. This consciousness is what keeps the body alive and allows it to heal, so long as the illness or injury is not too serious."

Father Parrot continued, "This evening I asked the medic to remind Tully that if he would rest and keep his thoughts on God, it would relieve his anxiety and help his body heal."

"Wow," said Osmund the Otter, "I have never heard of anything like this before. In the past, when I have stood on a rock and looked down into the water to see my reflection, I have always said to myself, 'There I am. That's me. I am a river otter.' When I see my reflection from now on I am going to say, 'There is the body that I move around in, see with, smell with and learn with. I am the spirit soul who lives inside this body.'"

"Very good, you are a fast learner," said Father Parrot. "We are all going to learn that we are not our bodies, and we are not even our minds or brains. This is very important for us to understand, and we will learn more about it soon. But this evening I will teach you about the spiritual world that existed before the beginning of our universe.

"The title of tonight's story is 'The Spiritual Sky,'" announced Father Parrot. "I would like for everyone here to close their eyes for a few moments and imagine a beautiful planet where Krishna is sweetly playing His flute.

"Not fair," said Father Parrot. "You two young groundhogs are peeking. I need all of you to close your eyes for a few minutes and meditate on this image."

As soon as Father Parrot saw that everyone had their eyes closed, he again asked that they try to imagine Krishna standing on the wonderful planet called Goloka Vrindavan. "Now," said Father Parrot, "let yourself imagine the most powerful and beautiful light shining from His body. This light is alive and it can think. It lights up the entire spiritual world."

"Yes," whispered Sarah the Swan, "I see it. I am getting chills. This is so splendid."

Others could be heard quietly saying, "Yes, I see it also."

"This magnificent light is one of Krishna's many wonderful powers," Father Parrot explained, "and it has a special name. It is called the *brahmajyoti.*

"Now," he continued, "keep your eyes closed for a few more minutes and imagine an enormous spiritual sky all around Krishna's planet. Do you see the millions and millions of planets floating in this spiritual light? These spiritual planets are called Vaikuntha planets."

Another question came from the cliff-top. "Are these Vaikuntha planets like our planet?"

"No," said Father Parrot. "These are spiritual planets, not material planets like the earth we live on. And because they are completely spiritual, they are alive and can think, as well as communicate. Vaikuntha means 'that place which is free from fear and worry.'"

Father Parrot instructed everyone to open their eyes.

Tavish and Taro, twin turtle brothers who were listening with their older sister, whispered to each other, "I wonder if this kind of spiritual knowledge is what we need to learn in order to become brave Veda Guardians."

GOLOKA VRINDAVAN

VAIKUNTHA PLANETS

Father Parrot, who overheard their comment, said, "Not only do the Veda Guardians have to learn this sacred knowledge before they become regional Veda Guardians, they also have to study with Old Gray Elk so that they are able to clearly understand what is good and what is evil."

"Wow!" said Tavish and Taro. As Father Parrot looked around he could see many young animals straightening up at the thought of becoming Veda Guardians.

Seeing their enthusiasm, Father Parrot realized that he needed to begin telling the forest animals something very, very important for their spiritual understanding. "Students studying to be Veda Guardians," he said, "are taught that they cannot be given such high and secret teachings unless they understand that they are servants of God. It is important that none of you ever desires to become a Veda Guardian in order to seek power and fame; your only intentions should be to serve and help others. All true Veda Guardians live by their two-worded motto, 'serve Krishna.'"

Father Parrot then continued, "As I told you earlier, floating in the *brahmajyoti*, the shining light that comes from Krishna's body, are millions and millions of Vaikuntha planets. On every Vaikuntha planet lives an expansion of Krishna Himself, called Narayan. Krishna is able to expand Himself into a splendid, four-armed form by His wonderful mystic power. The devotees living on each Vaikuntha planet love and respectfully worship Narayan."

Father Beaver, who had been raising his paw, said, "It seems hard to believe that God can expand Himself into so many Narayan forms and on so many Vaikuntha planets."

"You're right," said Father Parrot, "it is difficult, unless we are given examples to assist our imaginations. In all the sacred scriptures found in our world it is said that God is everywhere and is all-powerful.

"A short time ago," Father Parrot revealed, "I flew over to Blue Bay Village and watched through a window as the humans living there appeared to be glued to something they call a television. The television looked like a box with tiny people inside talking to one another. I was amazed as I heard one human say to another, 'Just think, there are millions of other humans all over our planet who are watching this very same movie tonight.'

"I realized," said Father Parrot, "that the picture in one movie had been multiplied so that it could be seen in millions of homes around our world. It occurred to me that if the pictures in one movie could appear at the same time in all those homes around the world, then the all-powerful God can easily expand Himself into a Narayan form on each of the Vaikuntha planets."

"As I had my eyes closed," said Billy the Bluebird, "I was able to see many planets floating in the spiritual sky. I saw them floating in the *brahmajyoti*, the bodily rays of Krishna."

"Yes," said Father Parrot, "very insightful. Please also remember that in the spiritual world there is no fear of other living beings because everyone has a pure and loving heart. In addition, there is no birth, death, old age or disease."

Then Father Parrot told the animals that it would be better to meet once a week, starting next Sunday evening, so they'd have plenty of time to ponder the Krishna stories and discuss them with their families and friends. "Besides," he said, "everyone is so busy during the week, it would be easier to meet together on Sundays."

Father Parrot closed the meeting on a happy, personal note, announcing that his three young children would begin flying lessons the next morning, and that by the following Sunday evening they might be ready to fly to the clover field for the Krishna story hour.

He also reminded them that Mother Raccoon had brought some delicious berries for them to eat, and he wished his forest friends a safe trip home, saying to all, "Good evening!"

And all of the animals replied, "Good evening!"

Fourteen Tigers

Chapter Five

Powerful storm winds were blowing in from the west.

Ordinarily the Bay Ridge Mountains were high enough to break up strong winds before they reached Tiger Tooth Valley or the Tiger Ridge Mountains; but today was different. By late morning, rain had soaked the valley and was soon pounding on the Tiger Ridge Mountains. The green grasslands, bushes and thick forests of the foothills were lashed so hard by wind and rain that the trees were bending to the breaking point. But no such weather was going to stop Father and Mother Tiger from crossing the mountain range between them and Tamel Forest to see their wounded cub, Tully.

During the night several hours earlier, Danbar the Falcon had updated the worried parents about their cub's improved condition; but they were still very concerned and were missing their youngster terribly. Six other white tiger couples accompanied them to Tamel Forest. The striped friends traveled with the anxious parents to support them in any way they could. They wanted Tully's parents to know that the tiger community cared about their family.

As the fourteen felines traveled down the mountain trail, Father Raccoon called his children to have a look. They gazed in wonder at the magnificent travelers: the graceful and largest members of the cat family and some of the fastest runners in the Northwest Region.

"Look how many there are!" exclaimed Ruben the Raccoon, as the sure-footed cats entered Tamel Forest.

"This is a wonderful sight," said Mother Raccoon joining them. "There must be a dozen or more tigers in all. I've never seen such a long parade of these marvelous creatures."

Damp but determined, the tiger friends waited in the clearing outside the Tamel Forest clinic, while the tiger parents prepared to visit their wounded cub. Understanding that their appearance would attract a crowd of Tamel Forest animals, waiting tigers formed a protective circle at the entrance to the clinic to provide Tully and his parents maximum privacy.

The chief medic deer greeted Father and Mother Tiger. She told them their baby was doing much better and that by the next morning the deer medics planned to have him stand and take a few steps. "If all goes well," she told them, "your cub will be able to travel home in a few short weeks." This was good news to the tiger parents, who had to resist the urge to run straight into the clinic to embrace their son.

Mother Tiger entered the clinic quietly. Due to her large size and strength she had to be very careful not to knock over and damage anything in the room. As she bent down to kiss her cub, he opened his eyes. "Mother!" he purred loudly, "I'm so glad you're here."

"Your father and I have missed you so much," said Mother Tiger. "He is right behind me."

Tully lifted his head as his father arrived and nuzzled his son's face. "I'm so glad . . ." Tully said, dropping back on the pillow, too weak to finish.

"That's all right, son," Father Tiger whispered. "Don't try to talk."

Rather than ask the tiger parents to leave so their cub could rest, the chief medic deer suggested they remain by his side for awhile and speak quietly to him about their love for him and their assurance that he would get well soon. "He's so glad you're here," said the medic, "your closeness will make his rest more healing."

With this, Mother Tiger told her little cub, "You can probably smell that our fur is damp. That's because we walked through quite a rainstorm as we crossed the Tiger Ridge Mountains this morning to visit you." She then gently licked the top of his head.

After a few moments, Father Tiger said, "Your little brother and your friends want you to get well quickly. They said they missed you last night during their puddle dodge game under the moon."

Tully had a little strength left to squeak out a question: "Father, is the hunter who shot me with his bow and arrow still around?"

Understanding that his son was afraid that the hunter might be lurking in the forest waiting for him, Father Tiger moved closer to reassure his cub. "Tully," he said, "listen to me carefully. The mountain lions found the hunter this morning hiding in the Bay Ridge Mountains." The loving father tiger held back a snarl meant for the hunter. "They captured him and are holding him until one of the regional Veda Guardians takes him to where he can be judged for what he has done. You are entirely safe here in the Tamel Forest clinic."

"Our mountain lion cousins are very carefully patrolling the Bay Ridge Mountains," Mother Tiger added, "especially where the river runs through. They will not permit another hunter to enter their mountains."

"And," said Father Tiger, "your uncle has gotten hundreds of white tigers to spend more time guarding the mountains near our home, so that you can play freely when you return."

Tully smiled in a way that made clear how protected he felt. He began to fall asleep as Mother Tiger hummed a favorite song in his ear. Outside, every type of animal was gathering near the clinic. Most of them had never seen such a crowd: a dozen huge tigers, with their large heads, bright blue eyes and long, sharp teeth. The Tamel Forest creatures were awed by the tigers' smooth but powerful movements.

After dozing off briefly, Tully opened his eyes and said, "Mother, would you tell me more about the home of Krishna?"

Mother Tiger knew that her cub loved to hear about Krishna. Every chance Tully got, he asked his mother and father to tell him stories about Krishna and the planet where He lives.

Mother Tiger started speaking softly and soothingly to her son: "There are twelve large forests on Goloka Vrindavan, the topmost planet in the spiritual world. These forests are overseen by the lovely goddess named Vrinda Devi. There is a river on Goloka Vrindavan called the Yamuna River that flows through the twelve forests.

"In the five forests that face the Yamuna River's eastern shore lives a very special person: Balaram, the elder brother of Krishna. The two brothers enjoy playing together in the forests along with Their friends, the cowherd boys. The activities that Krishna and His friends enjoy are called pastimes."

Mother Tiger licked the face and ears of her baby before continuing. "On the west bank of the Yamuna River are seven forests that Krishna also enjoys. These forests have many mango trees with blossoms that smell so sweetly they attract happy bumblebees from all over Vrindavan. The trees in the forests continually sway in softly blowing breezes that arrive from the Malaya Hills."

Mother Tiger noticed that a peaceful, healing sleep had crept over her cub. As she looked around she saw that the chief medic deer had been standing behind her, listening. The medic apologized for eavesdropping, saying that since Father Parrot had begun telling the Tamel Forest animals about Krishna, she just couldn't help listening in. She then asked Mother Tiger, politely, if she might have time to finish describing for her the forests of Goloka Vrindavan.

"I'd be happy to," said Mother Tiger, checking again to see if Tully really was asleep. "Of the twelve forests, one is considered the most special: it is called Vrindavan Forest. This is the place where Krishna, Balaram and the cowherd boys play in the most enchanting areas."

The medic deer then whispered a question: "Please tell me, Mother Tiger, what's a demigod?" Although her question had nothing to do with Mother Tiger's description, she had heard about demigods from Winslow the Owl; and she desperately wanted to know who the demigods were.

Mother Tiger nodded and said, "Demigods are living beings like us who have become especially faithful devotees of Krishna. They live on magnificent planets in this material world where they worship the Lord with love and devotion. However, our goal should be to reach Goloka Vrindavan, where Krishna resides. His presence makes it even more glorious than the topmost heavenly planets of this universe."

The medic deer thanked Mother Tiger for answering her question and for speaking so knowledgeably about Krishna and His spiritual planet, Goloka Vrindavan.

"You're welcome," said Mother Tiger sincerely.

Then Father and Mother Tiger both crouched down and kissed Tully, waking him. "We have to leave you for today so you can rest and heal," said Father Tiger.

"We must go and let your brother know how you're doing," added Mother Tiger.

"We all will be together soon," they both promised, licking their little wounded cub one last time.

At the clinic door, the two tiger parents thanked the chief medic deer who reminded them that their cub would continue to receive the best care possible.

The clouds had scattered, the bright sun was shining and cool breezes had dried the foliage. The forest felt happy again, as the fourteen majestic tigers strode quickly up the trail toward their home in the Tiger Ridge Mountains.

The Veda Guardian
Chapter Six

"What was that?" Tully the wounded tiger cub asked. He had spent most of yesterday resting, remembering the comfort of his parents' visit, and had taken a few unsteady steps. This morning, he was feeling a little stronger and was quite awake. Father Parrot had entered the clinic and was talking to the chief medic about the cub's health, when the young tiger asked his question.

The medic turned to see if her patient was okay, but Father Parrot understood what Tully was talking about. "What you are hearing," said Father Parrot, "is the sound of elephants. Whenever a Veda Guardian nears a community, the elephants that carry their supplies start blowing their trunks—like trumpets—to notify the citizens that the guardian is arriving in the company of a golden eagle, a black leopard and three huge elephants."

The cub could hear the blasts echoing off the mountain ranges surrounding Tamel Forest. The medic said she had heard that the Veda Guardian would be passing through Tamel Forest on her way to pick up the hunter who had harmed the tiger cub.

When Tully heard this he said, "Oooooh," in a long, drawn-out manner.

Father Parrot hopped closer to the cub. "You appear to be much stronger today," he said smiling at the little tiger. Tully said that he missed his mother and father and was sorry he had gone to sleep in the middle of his mother's story about the planet where Krishna lives.

The medic told the mayor of Tamel Forest that the cub's parents seemed to know quite a bit about Goloka Vrindavan.

"Yes," Tully interjected. "My mother was telling me about the twelve forests on Goloka Vrindavan when I fell asleep . . . and something about a river."

"Well," said Father Parrot, "I can tell you more about that river if you would like me to."

"Please do," said the cub, as he rolled over to face the colorful bird. The chief medic leaned in closer to listen.

"The river is called by the name Yamuna Devi," said Father Parrot. "She is like a lovely sapphire necklace or a blue lotus garland winding her way through the center of Goloka Vrindavan's enchanted spiritual forests. Her shores are decorated with precious jewels of many colors. The waves can be heard chanting holy prayers. Swans, cranes and other birds also chant the holy names of God. Her water tastes as sweet as honey. Splendid jewel fish splash playfully in this water as birds fly overhead and decorate the sky."

"Tell me about the jewel fish," Tully begged, as goose bumps rose under his fur.

Father Parrot smiled, "The jewel fish swim in Yamuna Devi's water, and their bodies are made of many spiritual jewels that are completely alive. As the light shines through the water, the jewel fish glow with all the colors of the rainbow, and everyone who sees them—even peacocks—gazes in amazement at this dazzling display.

"Even the mountains and groves on Goloka Vrindavan," added Father Parrot, "wear a wide range of vivid colors. If you are not too tired, I could tell you a little more about them."

"Not tired! Not tired!" Tully exclaimed, exhibiting a small burst of energy. Thinking about Krishna and His wonderful home helped Tully take his mind off the pain of his healing wound.

It was easy to see that Father Parrot greatly enjoyed telling anyone and everyone about the wonders of Goloka Vrindavan.

"As you wade or swim in the Yamuna River, you can see in the distance the King of Mountains. It is Goloka Vrindavan's most majestic mountain, called Govardhan Hill. The rocks covering Govardhan Hill are actually precious jewels that serve as thrones, couches and other sitting places for Radharani and Krishna.

"The peacocks on Govardhan Hill dance joyfully. The bees hum and cuckoo birds sing melodiously, while other colorful birds chirp along sweetly." Tully and the chief medic deer could almost hear the music.

"There are many deep caves in the thick forests on Govardhan Hill. The *kadamba* trees and *madhavi* vines on the hill provide Krishna with brilliant flower blossoms and delicious fruits for His eternal pastimes with Radharani.

"Not far from Govardhan Hill are nine groves in which Krishna enjoys happy pastimes with His devotee friends. One grove is shaped like a giant lotus flower—a lovely flower that has many petals. This grove has seats made of gold, sapphires and rubies. In the middle of this grove stands a three-story temple, and from the top floor Krishna can see, in every direction, all the groves and forests of Goloka Vrindavan.

"The grove next to this one has sixteen tall trees, four in each corner—trees that have green, red, yellow and bluish-black flowers so vibrant and fragrant that bumblebees fly around them even at night." This amused Tully, the baby tiger. Night was the time tigers usually walked in the forest, and he'd never seen bees out at night.

"The third grove is very unique," continued Father Parrot. "In this grove the birds, bees and trees are of numerous colors, shapes and sizes.

"Near this grove is another grove made from moonstones and crystals. Everything there is white, including the cottages, sitting and resting places. Even the plants and animals are white." To the young tiger, this sounded like a great place for the white tigers in his family. Tully grinned as he imagined playing hide-and-seek in a white grove– until he remembered his stripes.

Father Parrot went on to describe several more wonderfully colored groves, including one in which everything (even the soil, birds and trees) is a brilliant golden color–the color of Radharani's complexion.

"Another grove is comprised of a deep blue color. The cottages and benches are all made with sapphires that create a captivating atmosphere," said Father Parrot. "It is a grove in which Lord Krishna, with His bluish hue, can blend in very easily." The kitten purred at the thought of his favorite game.

"And there is a red grove," said Father Parrot, "just like Krishna's handsome reddish palms. The leaves, flowers, swings and chairs are stunning shades of red. Even the ground is carpeted with sparkling rubies.

"The eighth grove is delightfully green-colored. The cottages, sitting places and paths are covered with designs made from radiant emeralds," explained Father Parrot. This grove really appealed to the chief medic deer who loved to snack on tender, green, low-hanging tree leaves.

Father Parrot then described the ninth and final grove to his engrossed audience. "At the center of the other eight groves sits one that resembles a floating lotus flower. Inside this grove is a temple decorated with emeralds, rubies and moonstones. This temple is shaped like a sixteen-petal lotus flower." Father Parrot stopped speaking at the end of this description, which was filled with beauty beyond the imagination.

After listening to Father Parrot's descriptions of the nine enchanting groves on Krishna's spiritual planet, Goloka Vrindavan, Tully switched abruptly to a relationship question that had been on his mind for quite some time.

"Does Krishna like to play with animals like us?" he asked.

"Certainly," said Father Parrot. "In fact, Krishna loves all of His animal friends in Goloka Vrindavan, and He enjoys playing with each of them. He even has pets like oxen, deer and parrots."

Being a deer herself, the chief medic couldn't help wondering what it would be like to be a pet on Goloka Vrindavan. "Does Radharani also have pets?" she asked Father Parrot.

"Yes, Radharani has pet cows that give large amounts of milk, and She uses it to cook for Krishna. She has a pet monkey, as well as a deer. She even has a pet elephant, a chakori bird, a calf, a swan and," Father Parrot paused and stood a little taller, "two pet parrots. The two birds love to tell jokes and keep everybody laughing."

Although Tully was eager to hear even more about Krishna, His spiritual planet and pastimes, due to his injury he began to feel sleepy and tired.

Suddenly there was a loud sound from the other side of the lake near The Willows. This was a good time for Father Parrot to assume his role of Tamel Forest mayor and investigate. The medic deer thanked Father Parrot for visiting; as the bird moved to leave and the tiger cub closed his eyes. Father Parrot's wings rapidly lifted him above the trees and over Beaver Lake toward The Willows.

From high above the lake, in a clearing near the great willow trees, Father Parrot saw three enormous elephants with ears that flapped like banana leaf fans. Each elephant's trunk was draped over one of its tusks. Two large cages were fastened on the back of one elephant, and three badgers rode inside one cage. The powerful looking mammals were covered with dirt from the tunnels where they were caught. The other cage was empty.

A black leopard trailed the elephants. Father Parrot saw him pause on a small rise, alert to any danger that might lie ahead. Although he could not see it, Father Parrot knew that somewhere up in the sky a golden eagle was watching over the traveling Veda Guardian. The grave responsibility of the leopard and eagle was to protect the Veda Guardian from any kind of danger.

The Veda Guardian was a strong black bear who stood a little over four feet at the shoulder. Her black fur was smooth and short with a large white "V" on her chest. Guardian Dova, the Veda Guardian, was respected by all for her vast knowledge of law and for being wise, fair, humble and pure. Due to her humility, Guardian Dova did not enjoy being the center of attention. She would usually get down from her seat on the elephant and walk whenever her party neared a group of animals.

Father Parrot descended and landed near the noise. He was relieved that Guardian Dova had arrived safely and that the commotion in The Willows was only an excited group of young Tamel Forest animals welcoming her.

"Welcome," said Father Parrot in his strong and friendly voice.

Peering through her eyeglasses at Father Parrot, Guardian Dova, in a business-like voice, said, "Good afternoon, Mayor Parrot, I think we will rest here for the night under the willow trees." (The guardian and her companions needed to cross the Tiger Ridge Mountains in time to camp in Tiger Tooth Valley the next evening–her last stop before reaching the Bay Ridge Mountains. There she would take custody of the hunter whose shooting of the tiger cub was against both the laws and the values of the territory.)

Father Parrot dropped down to a branch near Guardian Dova so they could speak comfortably to one another. They had met before, and the guardian graciously asked about Mother Parrot.

"She is doing well and enjoys mothering our three baby parrots who are just learning to fly," Father Parrot said with pleasure. The guardian took off her glasses, smiled and shook her head slowly from side to side, as she congratulated the proud father.

But the guardian was mostly serious, having an important matter on her mind. "As you know, I'm on my way to the Bay Ridge Mountains to pick up the hunter who shot a young cub in the Tiger Ridge Mountains."

"Yes," answered Father Parrot. "That would be Tully. I spent some time with him today. I'm happy to say that he is mending very nicely."

"That is positive news," said Guardian Dova. "I'm relieved to hear it."

Then she chuckled, "I've heard the animals want me to tell them a story, as I always do when I visit. After I rest a bit, I would like to tell them about something that took place in another part of the Northwest Region. I know it is short notice, but as mayor, could you arrange to have the Tamel Forest citizens meet here by The Willows in about two hours?"

"Certainly," said Father Parrot. "You may expect a large gathering. The Tamel Forest animals have been coming together in great numbers to hear stories about Krishna and His spiritual world."

"That is excellent," said Guardian Dova as she raised a heavy paw and turned toward her tent.

The lowering sun had begun to spread an orange tint over the clover field southeast of The Willows, when Chandler the Chipmunk turned to a friend and said, "Can you believe how many animals are already here?"

"Nothing like trumpeting elephants to gather a crowd," answered his friend.

The Fox Race

Chapter Seven

"Not long ago two close friends—a red mother fox and a gray mother fox—decided to take their kits on a picnic in the foothills of the Caribou Mountain Range. The five young kits—three red and two gray—were all best friends and loved to play together."

So began Guardian Dova, as she spoke to the Tamel Forest animals gathered in the clover field southeast of The Willows. Like all Veda Guardians, she was an expert storyteller who could tell stories that were so colorful and intriguing that the forest creatures would not miss an opportunity to hear one.

"The seven foxes climbed the Caribou trail until they reached a clearing well above the valley," Guardian Dova continued. "The red and gray fox mothers found a meadow where they could enjoy their lunches and watch their kits play.

"After finishing their meal, the five kits played a game to see who could jump the farthest and the highest. Not surprisingly," said Guardian Dova, "Bragdon, the largest gray kit (and perfectly named), began to brag that he could run faster than any of the other kits. He looked at Redmund, the largest of the red fox children, and boasted, 'I can run faster than you, and I can prove it.' Bragdon pointed to the tall tree at the far edge of the clearing, down a little hill, adding, 'I'll race you to that tree.'" Guardian Dova paused and looked over her audience. The youngsters were leaning forward with great interest.

"Redmund looked to the right where—way beyond the tree—he could see their home in Cave Maker Valley. 'You can't beat me,' he told Bragdon. 'I'm a fast runner too.'

"'Then let's race to the tree,'" challenged Bragdon, the gray fox.

"Well now," said Guardian Dova, "as you can imagine, there was great excitement among the three younger foxes at the thought of a race between their elder brothers. 'Who would win?' they wondered . . . and they worried a little as well.

"Although he didn't show it, Redmund was also nervous—about whether he could win; but he couldn't refuse Bragdon's challenge. 'All right,' he said a little shyly, 'I'll race you to that tree.'"

Guardian Dova explained how Bragdon placed a stick for the starting line. "One of the younger kits called out, 'Ready?' and Redmund and Bragdon dug their claws into the ground to get good traction for the start of the race.

"The moment of truth had now arrived," said the guardian. "Bragdon's younger sister, the official starter for the race, said, 'On your mark . . . get set . . .'"

"GO!" honked Grady the Goose, who had become overly excited listening to Guardian Dova's story.

Hearing this sudden shout from the crowd, the young animals rolled on the ground in laughter. Even the storyteller chuckled.

When the laughter had finally stopped, Guardian Dova resumed her description of the great race. "As we all now know," she smiled, "somebody yelled, 'Go,' and Bragdon and Redmund leaped forward, accelerating as fast as they could.

"Back under the shade of their picnic tree the two mother foxes were enjoying their lunch, good conversation and the fresh mountain air. Suddenly they stopped talking," Guardian Dova paused, "and noticed the great noise and excitement."

147

Guardian Dova continued, "What the mother foxes took in with a glance," she said, "filled them with motherly concern: their eldest kits racing at top speed down the hill across the clearing toward a very large tree at the edge of a steep cliff, with dangerous rocks, thorns and bushes below.

"Both mothers jumped to their feet and, in what sounded like a mix of barking and howling, they shouted, 'Stop! Stop now!'

"Since they were running downhill, and because they wanted to show how fast they could run, the two kits were racing faster than they had ever run before. The wind roared in their ears and made their eyes fill with tears."

"Guardian Dova must have enjoyed playing when she was a cub," thought Mother Parrot, looking over at the captivated youngsters, "to be able to tell the story with such realism."

"As the fox mothers watched the dangerous situation unfold, terrified that their racing kits would not be able to stop, they screamed even louder: 'Bragdon! Redmund! FALL NOW!!!'" Guardian Dova paused to let young imaginations run like the racing fox kits.

"Many thoughts can go through a young animal's mind in less than a second," said Guardian Dova. "When Bragdon heard the mothers yelling for them to stop, he laughed to himself and thought, 'If Redmund obeys his mother, I'll win for sure.' And he tried to run even faster.

"But when Redmund heard his mother shout, 'Fall now!' he thought, 'My mother has always taught me to obey her, even if I don't feel like it, and even if I don't understand why. I don't want to fall and lose this race, because Bragdon will brag and make me feel bad about myself. But I must obey my mother.' With that thought, he stopped moving his legs, which made him fall forward, tumble and roll a short distance until he bounced and slid painfully to a complete stop.

"When Redmund recovered from his tumble and looked up, he saw his mother and the gray fox mother running down the hill toward him with looks of great concern on their faces. However, they were not looking at him. He brushed himself off and got to his paws, a little surprised and disappointed," said Guardian Dova, "as the two mothers ran past him. Then he saw the reason why.

"'Oh my,' Redmund said to himself, as he followed the mothers to the edge of the precipice, 'I had no idea this cliff was here. I hope Bragdon didn't hurt himself.'

"'Bragdon!' cried the two mothers, as the smaller foxes ran up behind them, 'Can you hear us? Where are you? Are you okay?'

"You can imagine how relieved they were, especially Bragdon's mother," said Guardian Dova, "to hear a frightened cry from the bottom of the cliff: 'Mother, please help me. My leg hurts.'

"Usually," said Guardian Dova, "a mother is not happy to hear a cry of pain from her youngster, but in this case Bragdon's mother was so happy to hear his voice—which showed that he was still alive—that she started to cry with joy, as she struggled down the steep, rough cliff to help him.

"While the smaller foxes lay on their stomachs with their noses sticking out over the edge of the cliff, watching Bragdon's mother go to his aid, Redmund's mother hugged her eldest child saying, 'Thank goodness you obeyed me. I know it hurt when you fell down, but because you obeyed me, you didn't get hurt as much as Bragdon.'

"Since she was extremely relieved, and because she loved her child so much," said Guardian Dova, "when Bragdon's mother finally reached him, she gave him a big hug. 'I am so thankful that you are still alive,' she said. Usually Bragdon thought he was too old for that much mothering, but not this time.

"The red mother fox instructed the other kits to back away from the edge of the cliff and then started climbing down carefully to assist the gray mother fox. Together they lifted Bragdon out of the bush he was stuck in and helped him make his way back up to their picnic spot. With a cloth napkin they made a sling for his injured, left, front leg, cleaned each of his cuts and scrapes and then walked back down the Caribou Mountain Range's slope and home to Cave Maker Valley."

Guardian Dova described Bragdon's injuries. "He limped down the mountain trail staying close to his mother," she said. "He had wanted to show his sister and friends what a fast runner he was. Instead, he felt embarrassed and was hurting all over. Not only did he have a broken leg, but his whole body was covered with bruises, scrapes and cuts.

"After being very quiet for some time, he looked up at his mother and humbly said, 'I am so sorry I didn't obey you. Nothing was as important to me as winning the race and showing off, not even obeying you. I have learned my lesson, and I will never disobey you again.'"

Guardian Dova interrupted her story to point out that Bragdon's mother very much appreciated what her son said to her. "She stopped walking and bent down to give him another hug and kiss, saying, 'Your father and I love you and your sister more than anything else in the world, and we want the very best for you. I hope you will always remember the lesson you learned today on obedience.'"

Guardian Dova looked at the gathering of forest animals over the top of her glasses. "I am happy to report that Bragdon's leg and other injuries have healed, and he is a changed kit. He was so ashamed of his actions that he stopped bragging, and he obeys his mother and father even when he'd rather not."

The story was done. In closing, Guardian Dova said, "I am pleased to hear that your mayor (she meant Father Parrot) has begun teaching you the most secret knowledge about Krishna and His spiritual world. By learning and accepting these important spiritual teachings we will all grow to be better citizens of the forest."

Due to the amount of respect Mother Parrot had for Guardian Dova, she had come to hear her thoughtful story while Father Parrot stayed home with their triplets.

Mother Parrot had listened carefully to Guardian Dova from a sturdy tree limb with several other birds, so that she could tell her three baby parrots the story of the racing fox kits as soon as possible.

The Lunar Chant

Chapter Eight

Swimming beneath the water of Beaver Lake as easily as dolphins, the beaver kits joyfully played follow-the-leader. Beavers can hold their breath for a long time, and under Mother Beaver's watchful eye, the youngsters were able to enjoy long submerged swims beneath and around logs and rocks.

After two hot but happy days clearing the area where the temple was to be built, it felt refreshing for the beaver family to be back in the water.

Their water frolic worked up large appetites in the small beavers, and soon the kits gathered around Mother Beaver to complain that they were feeling famished. Since the kits had worked so hard, and were tired of leaves and clover, Mother Beaver decided they deserved a special treat. They were thrilled at the choices of willow, birch or poplar tree bark. They made it easy by agreeing on poplar.

"Follow me," said Mother Beaver. "I'll take you to the most delicious poplar trees you've ever tasted." She led them swimming upstream in one of many creeks that flowed into Beaver Lake.

When they reached the poplar grove, the beaver kits ate bark until their bellies were full. It tasted even better than they had remembered. However, because they did not want to miss any of Father Parrot's story time, they soon jumped into the water and swam quickly back to Beaver Lake.

As they approached their home in the middle of the lake, they dove from the surface like small submarines and disappeared. One by one they entered an underwater tunnel that led into the middle of their lodge. It felt good to be home.

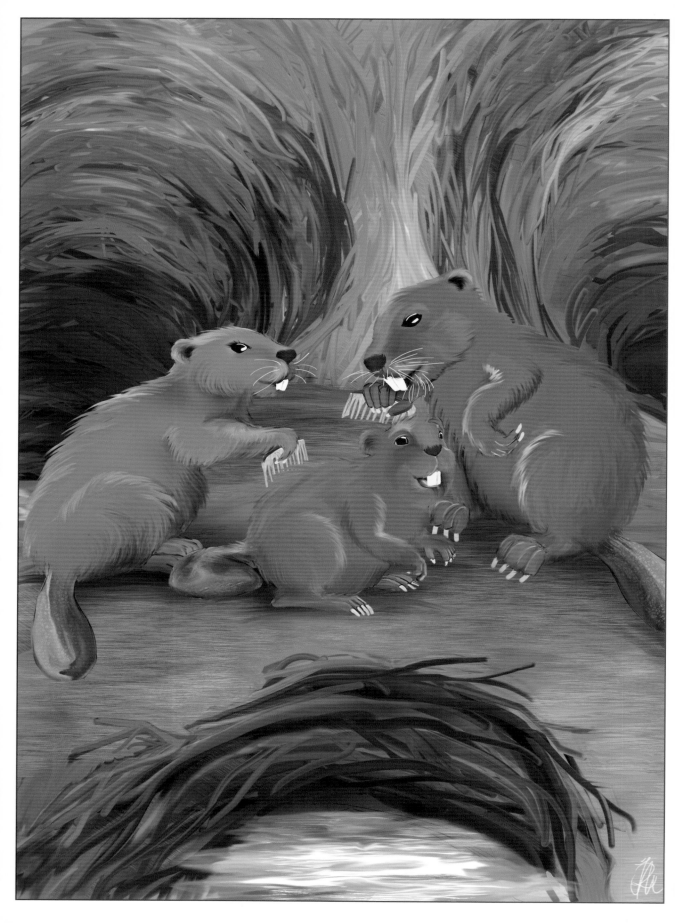

Father Beaver warmly greeted his returning family. Both parents gently combed their kits' fur in preparation for the meeting. They knew that Father Parrot had a lot to tell them this evening, and they wanted to hear every word.

Not far away birds and animals could be heard cheering the three young parrots—Penelope, Peter and Paul—as they launched from Parrot Pine to take their first flight out over Beaver Lake. They had spent several days trying small jumps and short flights. Now they were quite pleased with themselves as they extended their wings and flew over parts of Tamel Forest they used to see only from a distance. Below them, small groups of friends were walking to the meeting by The Willows.

"What's that sound?" Goldie, a small yellow hummingbird asked.

"I don't know," answered her blue hummingbird friend, Henrietta.

"Let's go find out," said Goldie.

They flew from their tree branch so fast that they looked like tiny flashes of color in the air. Soon they were flying around the meeting meadow by The Willows.

There they saw six chimpanzees, each standing behind one of six large kettledrums. Some of the chimps had brown hair; others were rust-colored.

As the hummingbirds hovered low, they saw Percival the Peacock and his wife, Pearl, standing close to the drums and dancing back and forth to the beats–"BOOM da da da, BOOM da da da, BOOM da da da, BOOM!"

"What an amazing rhythm," said Percival to the hummingbirds as they landed nearby. "Father Parrot has arranged for six of our chimpanzee friends to play the drums here each Sunday evening to alert the forest creatures that it is time to fill the clover field."

"Wow, this is exciting," said Henrietta the Hummingbird.

"My feathers are standing up all by themselves," giggled Goldie.

Percival laughed. "The chimpanzees will also play these drums at the end of tonight's meeting, when Father Parrot introduces a powerful chant to all the creatures of our forest."

"Let's go!" exclaimed Henrietta. "We have to make sure our friends get here on time." Flying in tight formation, the yellow and blue friends disappeared in a green blur.

As drumbeats continued to shake the meadow, the grassy clearing began to fill with creatures of every size, color and shape. Great excitement and energy filled the air.

Dropping from the sky, Father Parrot landed on a perch attached to a drum. He flapped his wings slowly to call for quiet. The drumming stopped, and the crowd became silent.

"As mayor of Tamel Forest," Father Parrot began, "I want to welcome a guest." This announcement was followed by a loud cheer from the crowd. All at once, a small, black-and-white bundle of fur bounded up onto the drum next to Father Parrot and took a shy bow.

The medic deer, who had pulled Tully on a travois to the gathering, cheered loudest of all. (When Tully had been told about the Krishna story meeting, he insisted on attending. His strong desire to hear Father Parrot's Krishna stories encouraged him to follow carefully the deer medics' instructions that helped heal his wounds.)

Pointing to Tully, Father Parrot said, "Let us give a very warm welcome to our special young guest, Tully the Tiger, from the Tiger Ridge Mountains."

Another roar went up from the crowd, with sincere shouts of "Welcome, Tully!"

Stepping back and forth a bit on his perch above the kettledrum, Father Parrot announced, "Friends, Mother Parrot and I are pleased to tell you that our children just earned their flying licenses—all three of them."

Shouts of "Bravo!" came from the crowd along with merry clapping, as the arriving Penelope, Peter and Paul hovered precariously for a moment on their way to the tree where Mother Parrot was perched.

"Practice makes perfect," Father Parrot cheered.

"Over to my left," he continued, pointing, "you may have noticed our river otter friend, Osmund, writing at that table as I speak. From now on he will be secretary at all our meetings writing down what is taught, along with your questions and my answers. Because of Osmund's service, the forest will have these stories, preserved on paper, to share with others who want to know the meaning and purpose of life." There was resounding applause for Osmund.

"This evening I would like to introduce to you a chant called the *maha-mantra*. *Maha-mantra* means, 'the great chant for deliverance.'" Father Parrot struck a thoughtful pose, "This chant is a prayer to Krishna and Mother Hara, who is also known by the names of Radharani and Hare. The *maha-mantra* is a cry to Radharani and Krishna, asking to always be engaged in Their devotional service.

"You already know that Krishna is the name for God—a name that means He is the most attractive person in all ways.

"A third name that you will hear in this chant is Rama. Rama is another name for Krishna that means He is the source of all happiness." Father Parrot spoke the names for Krishna with great reverence.

"As you listen to the chant this evening," he told the Tamel Forest audience, "always remember that Krishna and His dear most Radharani are present in Their names. When we chant the *maha-mantra*, it is said that Krishna is dancing on the tip of our tongue." He paused for a moment, giving his listeners time to ponder this concept that was still new to them.

"Chanting puts us directly in touch with Krishna. This closeness to Krishna makes us very happy." The audience could tell just from the way Father Parrot was speaking that what he was saying was very important.

"Krishna is God, the Supreme Person," Father Parrot said. "When we think of Him, He makes our minds and hearts very tender and receptive to His mercy. We then feel love for Him and yearn to serve Him in the spiritual world.

"For the last two days I have been practicing with our talented chimpanzee friends," Father Parrot said. "They will be playing the drums, other instruments and singing sweetly, as I teach you to chant the Hare Krishna *maha-mantra*. We will chant the entire *maha-mantra* and then ask you to chant along with us, over and over, until it comes to you naturally. Once each month we can all join in singing this chant that I have named 'The Lunar Chant,' because it is performed on the weekend of the full moon, which—you may not be surprised to hear—comes only once every month."

Father Parrot concluded his talk with an invitation: "After the chanting, you are all invited to a tasty vegetarian meal that has been cooked by the chipmunks, Mother Raccoon and eight of her close friends. When our temple is built, we will learn how to offer vegetarian food to Krishna. We will learn how offering food to Krishna turns it into spiritual food called *prasadam*, which means 'the Lord's mercy.'" Father Parrot brought his wing tips together to show his respect for Krishna.

Without warning, a roar from the kettledrums, that sounded like a thunderclap, was followed by the sounds of other musical instruments. This was a first for Tamel Forest. Soon the voices of the chimpanzees could be heard chanting together. Gradually the music grew louder and louder, as Father Parrot joined them in the chant.

The three baby parrots and all of their Tamel Forest friends, neighbors and family members listened intently as they chanted the *maha-mantra*:

Hare Krishna, Hare Krishna, Krishna Krishna, Hare Hare,

Hare Rama, Hare Rama, Rama Rama, Hare Hare.

Two very large, radiant, full moons illuminated the gathering of forest animals. One was sitting low in the evening sky, the other reflected on the waters of Beaver Lake. It was a sight—and a night—that no one would ever forget.

The moon rose slowly, casting a brilliant glow over the assembly, as the chimpanzees continued to lead the chant. The sweet smell of incense, made from forest roots and herbs, permeated the air. Father Parrot, with his head thrown back, sang the *maha-mantra* with a heartfelt desire to be with Krishna in the spiritual world. His loving chant to Krishna and Mother Hara, Radharani, was so moving that the other forest animals could not remain silent.

Soon they were clapping, dancing and chanting together with Father Parrot. As all of the animals continued to chant, they looked at one another with warm smiles on their glowing faces. By chanting the *maha-mantra*, they began to realize that they were not their physical bodies, but were individual spirit souls.

Even though their physical bodies were shaped differently from one another, the animals began to understand that they were spiritual children of the Supreme Father, Lord Krishna. A feeling of peace and happiness filled the animals of Tamel Forest. Their hearts and minds had never been so united.

Glossary

and

Pronunciation Guide

Balaram (BAH-lah-rom): the elder brother of Krishna.

Brahmajyoti (brah-muh-JOE-tee): the beautiful rays of light shining from the spiritual body of Krishna.

Dhoti (DOE-tee): a long cloth that covers the lower half of the body. It is worn by Krishna and His male devotee friends.

Goloka Vrindavan (go-LOW-kuh vrin-DAH-vun): the highest planet in the spiritual world where Krishna lives with His loving devotees.

Govardhan Hill (GO-ver-don hill): a large and splendid hill on Goloka Vrindavan. It is very dear to Krishna and His devotees who enjoy happy pastimes there.

Hare (HAH-ray): a name for Radharani, Krishna's most dear and loving companion.

Kadamba Trees (kuh-DUM-buh trees): trees that are usually seen in Vrindavan, having large, round, yellow flowers with a wonderful herbal aroma.

Krishna (KRISH-nuh): the original name of God. It means that He is the most attractive person in all ways.

Madhavi Vines (MOD-hah-vee vines): the beautiful vines that grow in Vrindavan, whose flowers are colorful and carry an indescribable sweet, spiritual fragrance.

Maha-mantra (MAH-hah MON-trah): the great chant to Mother Hara and Krishna asking to always be engaged in Their devotional service: "Hare Krishna, Hare Krishna, Krishna Krishna, Hare Hare, / Hare Rama, Hare Rama, Rama Rama, Hare Hare."

Malaya Hills (meh-LAY-uh hills): a group of hills not far from Vrindavan. These hills have many sandalwood trees that smell very fragrant.

Mother Hara (mother huh-RAH): a name for Radharani, Krishna's most dear and loving companion.

Narayan (nuh-RYE-uhn): a form of Krishna in the spiritual world. He has four arms, instead of two.

Prasadam (prah-SHAD-dum): vegetarian food that becomes spiritual after being offered to Krishna with love and devotion. Anyone who accepts Krishna's prasadam becomes pure-hearted, happy and devoted to Him.

Radharani (rod-hah-RAH-nee): Krishna's most dear and loving companion. She is Krishna's greatest devotee because no one loves Him more than She does.

Rama (RAH-muh): a name of Krishna that means that He is the source of all happiness.

Tulsi (TULL-see): a great devotee of Krishna in the form of a plant. She is very dear to Krishna, and her soft green leaves are offered to Him with love and devotion by His many devotees.

Vaikuntha (vie-KUN-thuh): the spiritual world, which is eternal and filled with wonderful happiness. It is far beyond this material world and is our original home.

Vina (VEE-nuh): a musical instrument with strings, played by devotees of Krishna in the spiritual and material worlds. It makes melodious sounds that are very pleasing to hear.

Vrinda Devi (VRIN-duh DAY-vee): the spiritual goddess who oversees Vrindavan. She helps arrange Krishna's happy pastimes with His devotees. She is a special devotee of Krishna, and the spiritual land of Vrindavan is named after her. The word Vrindavan means "The Forest of Vrinda Devi."

Yamuna River (yah-MOON-uh river): the beautiful, sacred river that flows through the many spiritual forests on Goloka Vrindavan. Krishna enjoys happy pastimes with His devotees in the waters and on the jeweled banks of this river. The Yamuna River is also called "Yamuna Devi." She, too, is a great devotee of Krishna.